Am I

disturbing

you?

Anne Hébert

Am I

disturbing

you?

Translated by Sheila Fischman

Published in 1999 by
House of Anansi Press Limited
34 Lesmill Road
Toronto, ON
M3B 2T6
Tel. (416) 445-3333
Fax. (416) 445-5967
www.anansi.ca

First published in French as *Est-ce que je
te dérange?* in 1998 by Éditions du Seuil

Distributed in Canada by
General Distribution Services Ltd.
325 Humber College Blvd.
Etobicoke, ON
M9W 7C3
Tel. (416) 213-1919
Fax (416) 213-1917
Email Customer.Service@ccmailgw.genpub.com

03   02   01   00   99   2   3   4   5   6

Canadian Cataloguing in Publication Data

Hébert, Anne, 1916–
[Est-ce que je te dérange? English]
Am I disturbing you?

Translation of: Est-ce que je te dérange?
ISBN 0-88784-640-8

I. Title   II. Title: Est-ce que je te dérange? English

PS8515.E16E8713   1999   C843'.54   C99-931350-9
PQ3919.H37E8713   1999

Cover design: Angel Guerra
Cover photo: Barnaby Hall

The Canada Council | Le Conseil des Arts
FOR THE ARTS | DU CANADA
SINCE 1957 | DEPUIS 1957

*We acknowledge for their financial support of our publishing program the
Canada Council for the Arts, the Ontario Arts Council, and the Government of
Canada through the Book Publishing Industry Development Program (BPIDP).
This book was made possible in part through
the Canada Council's translation grants program.*

Printed and bound in Canada

Am I

disturbing

you?

I

Delphine died in my bed last night, shortly before dawn. And I, Édouard Morel — a man without grace, and rather unsociable, too — have been forced to keep watch over her for a good while now, as if she'd been a woman dear to my heart. Now that the doctor has been advised, I just have to wait for them to carry her away.

She is here, stretched out on my unmade bed, the sheet pulled up to her chin, as I arranged it after I closed her eyes. I'd never noticed before how blue her eyes could be.

And now she is playing dead, conscientiously, unreservedly, as if she were at home, alone in the world, and with a kind of supreme wilfulness absorbing her entirely. I'm looking at her as I've never looked at her before. I exhaust myself looking at her. You'd think I was waiting for a sign from her, an explanation, the confession of a secret, whereas I know perfectly well that, right here before my eyes, she embarked upon an endless task, a ferocious and sacred one, and that no one will be able to distract her from it until she has turned to dust.

I swear, I'd stake my life on it, that this girl is nothing to me and she had no more reason to end her days here in my bed than anywhere else. She did it deliberately. I'm sure she did it deliberately. Considering how long she's been following me everywhere, clinging to my skin, gnawing at my bones.

"Am I disturbing you?"

The silence of death isn't altogether impenetrable then, for Delphine's voice persists in the muggy atmosphere of the closed room, tirelessly repeating her eternal, pointless question.

I've called the doctor, who is taking his time, and I've pulled the sheet over Delphine's face.

I've thrown open the shutters and I'm leaning out the window as far as I can. I seem to be looking for some kind of help in the grey dawn rising over the one tree in my building's tiny paved courtyard.

"Am I disturbing you?"

Scarcely a few hours ago. Her doleful, stubborn voice close to my ear. No doubt she'd kept a copy of my key, and she came in without making a sound. Her flat little Chinese shoes brushing the rough sisal of my rug. Suddenly she is there in the room where I'm asleep. She bends over me in the darkness as if she wants to force her way into my sleep, to interfere with my most secret dreams. Her long hair tickling my cheek, her breath racing on my neck.

She climbed the four flights of stairs without breaking the silence of the sleeping house. No witness to her light passage. Behind their closed doors all the tenants are asleep, ignoring one another in the dark as they do in the daylight.

Right away she starts to undress, her movements strangely slow, as if each article of clothing were wrenching away her soul.

Though I tell myself there's nothing all that unusual about some unimportant woman undressing at my place uninvited, just to annoy me, my attention is extreme, almost overcharged.

The faded jeans, the worn T-shirt, the frayed briefs fell around her untidily, onto the rug. When she was fully naked, standing in the middle of the room with everything that adorns, dresses, and covers tossed away from her, I knew that Delphine's pure nakedness, her devastating poverty, were intolerable to me.

She steps over her scattered garments with their sweetish smell, curls up under my blankets, sighs contentedly, and says it's as warm as if she were under the belly of a warm beast. She closes her eyes and seems to sleep right away. She talks as if in a dream:

"Sore feet. Sore legs. No money. Totally exhausted. Grandma's inheritance all gone. Too much walking. Days of it. Nights. Afraid to stop. Afraid of being killed where I stand. Taken by force. I'm insulted on the sidewalks as I walk along without stopping. Evil men stare at me as I pass, touch me with their dirty hands. Sore back. Sick to my stomach. As if I were pregnant again. Nothing to be done now. Nothing to say. Nothing to explain. Nothing to laugh at. Nothing to cry over. Nothing to eat, either. Only myself, all alone. Myself, less than nothing. Myself, and I've been walking for days. For nights. Thirst. For a good ten minutes I follow close behind a man who is eating grapes and spitting their skins onto the sidewalk. I eat the skins of the grapes spat out by the man who's walking down the street ahead of me. My stomach aches. Everything aches. The poor little thing who aches all over, as my grandmother used to say."

Delphine's usual chatter, inexhaustible. Herself, always herself, reflected in a mirror that is itself reflected in another mirror, and so on from mirror to mirror till her head spins, while Delphine's voice dwindles away. Pointless to prick up my ears. The bits of phrases that I hear suffice and I can't stand them.

An odd little laugh at the very back of her throat quavers like a sleigh-bell.

"I ripped off some shampoo at the supermarket."

I approach the bed, wanting to make Delphine feel ashamed about the grapes on the sidewalk and the stolen shampoo.

She moves her head and her hair falls onto her cheeks and her nose, long black threads. She talks and gets winded, lifts locks of hair with every breath, every word she utters. Doesn't even try to toss it off her face. Says she's just washed it, in the fountain in Place Saint-Sulpice.

"My hair's the only thing I love."

She tries to laugh again. Shows her teeth. Props herself up on the pillows. Raises her arms above her head. Her small breasts are flattened, disappear altogether. Her ribs become visible. I can't help thinking of the skeleton of a little ship in distress, washed up on my bed.

Delphine is stubborn; she resumes her monologue, seems to be trying to thumb her nose at some invisible person who's hidden in the bedroom, who would force her to get it all out very quickly — everything she's never said or even imagined saying to anyone.

I talk to her about her country, which she should never have left.

She replies:

"I have no country. My country is any city that has sidewalks where I can walk. Railway stations. Trains. Hotels. Airports. When I can follow someone everywhere. Shadow him. Wait till he turns around. To see me and be seen by me. In the hope that he'll take me home and adopt me. The way my grandmother came to my parents' house to get me the first time I nearly died. The last time, it was on account of Patrick Chemin and my child who is dead and gone now."

She goes on talking, chewing away at her words, while I'm no longer sure I can hear anything she says. In any case, I refuse Delphine, body and soul, and I haven't finished protesting her presence in my bed.

Now she is pronouncing my name slowly, distinctly, as if she were taking pains to decipher something strange that was written on the wall in front of her.

"Édouard, dear Édouard, let me sleep here. Only sleep. One more time. Only once."

She says again, echoing her own voice:

"Sleep. Sleep."

I lean over the untidy bed. I move her hair off her face, which is changing. Delphine's last sigh runs over my fingers, between the long locks of her black hair.

D octor Jacquet moves slowly, like someone who has
been snatched from sleep. There's no end to his
examination of Delphine's body stretched out on my bed.
He grumbles as if this examination annoys him more than
anything else in the world. Seems not to believe what he
sees. He turns to me.

"Are you a relative?"

"No, just a friend."

My face, turned blue by my overnight beard, seems to hold
his attention as much as Delphine's overly white arms,
where he's straining to look for needle marks. Is he trying
to catch someone out, someone dead or alive, over this
incongruous death?

"Did she shoot up?"

"Not as far as I know."

"Was she suicidal?"

"Not to my knowledge."

"In short, you don't know very much about this person."

"That's right, not very much."

I think, *I do know a couple of things about her,* but I'm

not really sure what I mean by that and I remain silent.

Dr. Jacquet's broad, clean-shaven face betrays deadly boredom. Sitting at my work table, he pushes away my papers, then writes his report. He mentions permission to postpone burial and says a post-mortem is essential.

"I warn you. If you're interrogated, you'll have to be more precise about this person."

"Her name is Delphine and I've known her for a few months."

I repeat "a few months." I meditate on the word *month*, the word *day*, the word *year*, and on time in general. I try to find the secret relationship that may well exist between measurable time and the scandal of Delphine's death.

All at once, abruptly, I remember that Delphine has just turned twenty-three. I've been thirty for two months now.

Two men in white smocks came to get Delphine. They took her to the place where dead girls are opened and emptied, and their hearts are weighed in rubber-gloved hands.

Nothing else to report. Leaning on the windowsill, I wait for the day to arrive altogether before I turn around to face the untidy room at my back.

The deserted courtyard is gradually waking. Cheeping of birds. Clatter of shutters thrown open. Broad shafts of soft September light. Through bursts of ringing bells I hear the streaming of the fountain at the church of Saint-Sulpice.

The sun is high now. It penetrates everywhere in the room, sheds violent light on last night's disorder, which is frozen in its tumult like the hands on a watch that has stopped.

Gather up Delphine's things, scattered all over the room. Make a tidy package of them. Change my soiled sheets. Pull the plaid blanket tight, without a crease. Sweep. Dust. Erase all fingerprints but my own. Chase away the shadow of

Delphine's fingers on any object they have touched. Let in lots of air between kitchen and bedroom. Alone once more. Pick up the thread of some copy I started last night. Line up words underneath realistic colour photos. Push mass-produced furniture for a mail-order catalogue. I'm used to it, though my aversion is intact.

"Mini-price. Maxi-quality. Guaranteed value. Super-sturdy. Multi-purpose. Melamine-surfaced particle board."

The term *melamine-surfaced* delights me, as if at one stroke I've achieved the most grotesque perfection of my soul.

Glued to my table. Move on from the convertible banquette to the stylized Louis XIV living room suite. Wait for the day to end. Act as if Delphine's bird-claws had never settled on me.

II

Who was the first, Stéphane or me, to notice Delphine beside the fountain, in the glow of the pink chestnut trees that line the square? Afterwards, that would prove to be a lively topic of conversation between Stéphane and me.

There was a girl who hadn't moved for quite a while, who was sitting on the rim of the fountain with the water streaming at her back. There was something surprising about her stillness. From her entire little person there emanated a kind of obstinacy at being there in the mist from the fountain, an unwillingness to exist anywhere else — elbows on her knees, folded in on herself, slightly shocked at finding herself in the world.

She sees two young men coming towards her, one stocky and dark, the other lanky and fair, and she acts as if she sees no one. Is it Stéphane? Is it me? One of us asks:

"Can we do anything for you?"

She doesn't reply right away, as if it were difficult for the question to make its way into her stony stillness. Her eyes looking up at us, open too wide, as blank as a statue's.

I repeat — this time I'm sure it's me:

"Can we do anything for you?"

We hear her voice, reluctant and remote, murmuring as if from the bottom of a well:

"If you want."

Stéphane and I take hold of her under the arms and pull her up. She doesn't resist and says:

"Thanks. But you really didn't have to."

And she worries about her baggage.

Once she was on her feet, her dress pink, as if the colour of the chestnut trees were rubbing off on her, we saw that she was pregnant.

She smooths her rumpled dress and her big belly with hands like a child's, slender and white. She speaks with excessive, nearly unbearable softness.

"The Fat Lady mustn't know I'm in Paris."

Just then the bells of Saint-Sulpice unfurl onto the square like an equinoctial tide, loud and joyous.

She smiles and tells us it's the angelus.

After she's settled on a café terrace in the square, she goes on looking at the fountain she's just left.

I point out that her coffee's getting cold, that she should drink it.

She takes a few sips, makes a face, pushes the cup away, says it's too strong and makes her feel sick to her stomach.

Stéphane offers her some tea, and she drinks it with a lot of milk.

She acts as if she's not with us and gazes attentively at the women who walk by. She stares at them. Knits her brow. Disparages them to her heart's content. None of them finds favour in her eyes. There's not one woman parading in the square who isn't caught in the act of resembling the Fat Lady.

"Too fat. Really thick. Too big. Wouldn't get through the door. Arms like boas. Legs like tree trunks. Above all, too old. Oh my, old, old, old enough to die. She ought to make room for the young."

She leans on the table, puts her head on her arms and cries.

I wish I weren't there, across from Delphine, when she's

crying. Stéphane offers her some cake.

She eats and she cries.

With her mouth full, she tells us that the Fat Lady must be somewhere in the city and that she absolutely has to be found, without her knowing it, and stopped from doing any harm. As for Patrick, he won't be here till tomorrow.

I ask who Patrick is.

She stands up and points to her big belly.

"Patrick, Patrick Chemin, sales rep, fishing tackle, he did this to me."

She slowly strokes her belly.

She sits again and gulps down the rest of her tea.

Then Stéphane steps in:

"And the Fat Lady, who's she?"

"Patrick's wife."

Exhausted by these confidences, reproaching herself for divulging them, she is absorbed for a moment in her desolation; then in a flash she fixes both of us, from across the table, with a look that seems not to belong to her, a look as sharp and cutting as a blade.

"What's most disgusting in this whole business is Patrick."

She falls silent at once, having reached the limit of what you can say and show in a glance without dying of shame.

She turns towards the fountain again, as if some reassurance could come to her from the streaming water. All around us, the murmur of the city has grown so loud that we can no longer hear the murmuring water.

And now a little voice, high-pitched, soft, sounding almost worldly, emerges from the scraping of chairs being pulled or pushed, the clink of glasses, the orders shouted or whispered, from the mingled conversations, the clatter of cars and buses.

She says:

"I'm Delphine."

She points to each of us in turn. Touches Stéphane and me on the chest, the shoulder.

"And you? And you?"

Our first names, which we offer immediately, seem to surprise her, to put her into a strangely joyous state more worrisome than her tears.

She repeats after us:

"Édouard. Stéphane. That's great. That's funny. Fantastic."

During her brief time among us, the list of names that sounded so joyously in Delphine's ear would hardly be longer than that, going from Patrick to the Fat Lady — if that Lady had a first name.

A side from the fireplace and the logs piled next to it, the table littered with papers, the two straw-bottomed chairs, and, in the place of honour, the double bed — usually only half occupied — there's nothing here.

I read and I work, I sleep and I eat, I drink, I wash and shave. Twenty metres square. Whitewashed. Lime wash with a tinge of blue, like a country dairy. There's no one here but me and my passing shadows reflected on the bare walls as the days go by. I myself cast a shadow on the white all around, as if I were a thick tree, a kind of dense spruce, from root to head. Myself to infinity. Just me repeated on the walls, the ceiling, on the creaking hardwood floor. My own memories flutter like moths in the room. Always the same, devoid of interest. My everyday movements here, near Place Saint-Sulpice, fourth floor, over-looking the courtyard. A studio apartment twenty metres square. Enough room to live and die without making a sound. No strict, pure angel, his crumpled wings grey, rust, and brown like those of a partridge, stands behind my chair and blames me. I am free, if I want, to be nothing and no one.

Above all, let her not come here to mix her traces with my own. Let there be no memory of her within these walls.

She was there next to the fountain, like a little heap fallen from the pink trees, half girl, half plant, like a swollen bunch of grapes. Her round belly. Her wrinkled dress. And I'll probably never know whether this creature is opposed to me or not.

Her image is too fresh. Without past or patina. Only from yesterday. Thin. Without depth. Leaving no trace on me, like distemper drowned in water on a smooth wall. Not deserving to live inside me, like the signs of my own passage. Pathetic Delphine, swallowed up at once by me, sole master of my dark memory.

Too many glimmers, too many spots of sunlight still persist in my eyes. No doubt they come from spending too long, yesterday, looking at the chestnut trees in the square.

P ale, thin, and long — like me, a specialist in little dead-end jobs — Stéphane experienced incredible ecstasies while listening to Bach and Mozart. His face then resembled those of the saints captured in mystical mid-prayer by painters of bygone days.

Very quickly his face came to bear the same expression when he looked at Delphine, who didn't look away; she was not at all uneasy under Stéphane's gaze, being fully taken up with herself, untangling the inextricable.

Around noon the next day, she turned up at his place on Rue des Anglais. Hadn't he given her his address and phone number?

He thinks:

Good God, I haven't made the bed, there are crumbs everywhere, my records on the floor . . .

She says:

"Patrick's plane has been rerouted to Marseilles because of the fog."

He thinks:

My God, what a mess, she turns up at my place out of the blue, on Sunday of all days, and I've slept in as I always do on Sunday, dirty shirt on the chair, socks on the floor, on the glazed tiles, my room a disaster, what will she think of me?

She says:

"I came to ask what I have to do to get to Marseilles."

He rubs his eyes. Explains that Marseilles is far away and that once the passengers are off the plane they will most likely be put on a train to Paris.

She wants to know what train, what station, and she's afraid the Fat Lady knows much more about it than she does, that she'll be the only one able to greet Patrick Chemin when he arrives in Paris.

He thinks:

Not here, I don't want her here, not today, I'm not ready for that, it's too small here, too dark, my room under the rooftop, the neighbours' dormer window right across from mine, my neighbours and I look at each other every chance we get, gimlet-eyed, like fighting cocks, and here she is in the middle of my room, so visible with her pink dress and her big belly, in a little while they'll see her too, those malevolent neighbours, they'll think she's an ordinary person paying an ordinary visit, but she's a marvel, my extraordinary guest.

She says again that Patrick Chemin's plane is lost in the fog. She's on the verge of tears.

Craning her neck, she looks out the window, the sky barely visible high above the narrow courtyard, a well of black light rather than a courtyard. She thinks she can hear the murmur of the sky above the rooftops.

"His plane. That's his plane. I'm sure it's his plane. I can hear it roaring and circling in the sky. I can hear it using up its fuel by going around so much, like a bumblebee, in that thick milkiness in the sky. This morning everybody was looking up at that sound. Even the Fat Lady was afraid it would burn up all its fuel, and fall and crash at our feet. The Fat Lady was frozen there like a statue. Like everyone else, for once. You could see that her big fingers were no longer moving on the yellow book she was reading. In the end, we were told the plane would land in Marseilles. So I came to find out what I have to do to get there."

He phones. But all the lines that have anything to do with Patrick Chemin's plane have been busy since morning.

She says again, "Marseilles." Swallows. Gathers momentum, and disjointed words tumble off her tongue — "Patrick Chemin," "airplane," "fog," "Fat Lady." The rest is as muddled as the tears on her cheeks, which she wipes away with her sleeve.

But now Stéphane must lend an ear to what is new in Delphine's confused remarks.

She talks about her grandmother, who died and left her an inheritance. She says she'll spend that inheritance, penny by penny, to travel, to follow Patrick Chemin to the ends of the earth if she has to.

She pronounces "grandmother" slowly, cautiously, as if it were a precious, fragile word, and her face lights up. Again she emphasizes the syllables in "grandmother," and she is absolutely happy.

"Do you want to see my inheritance, Stéphane dear?"

She pulls up her dress. He can see her Petit Bateau underpants. She undoes the little brown leather pouch that she's fastened around her waist with a belt against her bare skin. Shows him the coins and bills. Scatters them around her in the room. Then she runs to pick them up, like a hen picking at grain scattered in a barnyard.

Not knowing what to do with Delphine, who had started crying again, Stéphane brought her to my place, holding her hand all the way along the boulevard.

Later he would tell me all about Delphine's intrusion into his place, about the route they'd taken through the city.

He'd assure me that she'd neither seen nor heard anything around her. The new leaves at the tops of the trees, the scaly trunks of the plane trees, the song of the invisible bird, the round grilles at the foot of the trees, the captive roots beneath them, the light mist everywhere, the great murmur of midday, the busy passersby — life, all of life, had rained onto her and she hadn't been aware of it; she had shed it as a duck's back sheds water.

Once they reached Rue Bonaparte, outside my building, she cast away any trace of absence or daydream. All at once she dropped Stéphane's hand, surprised she'd held it for so long. Suddenly clear and precise, with no hesitation, she declared:

"Poor Stéphane, your hands are wet."

Very quickly she was standing in my doorway, saying, "Bonjour." And then Delphine walked into my place for the first time.

S he's out of breath and she looks bigger to me than she did yesterday. She sits on my bed. Piles the pillows behind her back. All her attention is devoted to recovering her breath and settling in comfortably. Delphine is at my place but it's as if she weren't here, she's facing me as if I didn't exist.

Then, abruptly, she springs to her feet and comes to stand next to me.

"I have to know. What station? What train? What time? Hurry, Édouard dear, please. Or I'll die right here, right now, on the ground at your feet."

Immediately I abandon my scattered papers, my catalogues and dictionaries. I pick up the phone. After listening to bursts of soft music for a long time, I finally get the information Delphine is waiting for.

She repeats after me, ten times at least, as if she were singing:

"Four p.m., Gare de Lyon, four p.m., Gare de Lyon, Gare de Lyon, four p.m., four p.m. . . . ."

Stéphane and I decided to show Delphine around the city while we were waiting for the train from Marseilles. The three of us walking. The mocking expression of some passersby. Which of the two of us is the father of that child who is practically visible through its mother's pink dress?

She already likes the *bateaux-mouches* and the banks of the Seine. She shuns monuments and museums like a child who's afraid of grown-ups. Despite the hazy day, like a December morning, we take her to the banks of the river. Her round belly thrust forcefully ahead of her seems not to belong to her, she is still so slender and frail, separated from her burden by steadfast childhood.

She's careful not to stumble on the paving stones. Then she sits on the ground, her back against the stone wall, despite our protests. The dampness doesn't bother her, or the cold stones.

Delphine looks at the Seine stretching out before her.

A white mist rises from the water. We can see the boats through the mist. At times half visible in the white mist. The lights of the *bateaux-mouches* slice through the fog in long luminous beams, and we hear them glide along the water. As if it were night.

She says:

"At my grandmother's house there's a river running nearby. Sometimes it runs through white mist, other times it's very bright because of the sun shining on it. I like it when my grandmother is rocking on the verandah. When she died, the rocking chair kept going back and forth in the wind all by itself, and I couldn't stand that rocking without my grandmother's slight weight. That rocking on the verandah drove me crazy and I ran down the road, carrying my inheritance against my belly, till I was out of breath, and then I met Patrick Chemin, who drove me to the nearest town."

Stéphane stands, I stand facing her, both of us shot through with mist, looking at her and listening to her, shivering as if it were winter though it's April already, while she sits on the ground, her back against the stone wall, her eyes vague, as if she's seeing her grandmother through the mist.

She says, suddenly very close, very alive, like someone stirring after a waking dream:

"Patrick and the Fat Lady haven't been married to each other for very long. It can't last. I'm pregnant. Patrick's real wife is me. He'll have to realize that."

On the bank in front of us is a man getting ready to fish. We watch him get ready. He sits on the paving stones, arranges his glittering metal line, rummages in a green plastic bucket.

Delphine assures us that the angler is poorly equipped as regards line and hook, and that he'll never catch anything.

"And besides, the Seine is rotten, everybody knows that."

She laughs, showing all her little white teeth. She points at us, at Stéphane and me.

"Little Frenchies, little Frenchies, your Seine is rotten!"

Stéphane clears his throat.

"And what about your river? What's your river like?"

"Wide and deep, with rapids. The Thibaud boy drowned in it, between the island and the mainland. The water was as black as hell."

The fisherman is standing in oversized trousers that hang loosely on his scrawny legs. He casts his shiny line onto water that recedes gently into the mist.

It's not possible that this girl has a grandmother like everyone else. A father, perhaps a mother? In vain I search her peculiar face for some sign of belonging, some slight trace of a resemblance. I look at her stretched out on the ground, propped up by the wall. Her pure stranger's mask positioned over the fine bones of her face. She has a touch of an accent. Pronounces her *a*'s like *o*'s and her *o*'s like *a*'s. Perhaps she's never lived in a real country, just in some hinterland known only to her, beyond sea and land, at the slender line between life and death.

"Let's get out of here. There's too much fog. We're getting all tangled in this cotton batting."

Delphine gets up and shakes out her dress, which is short in front, long in the back. Stéphane holds out his hand to her. He asks:

"Where do you come from?"

She points to the white sky above our heads, to a passing gull. Says, "Up there." Laughs.

"I took a plane to come here. My grandmother's inheritance was eaten up in one shot when I bought the plane ticket. One way. I'll be there when he arrives. The first one to greet him. Before the Fat Lady. Didn't see the Atlantic Ocean. Too many clouds. White. Thick. Just like meringue. Very white. Verging on blue. Dazzling. Flew too high. Didn't see the ocean. Cotton batting everywhere. There's no ocean. My mouth is full of cotton batting. I suffocate. Too high in the sky. The birds are dead. Too high to build nests. I'm coming, dear Patrick. Four p.m., Gare de Lyon. I'll be there. Before the Fat Lady."

The fisherman's line goes taut. A little fish is wriggling at the end of the line. The fisherman quivers with joy from head to toe.

Delphine declares that it's high time we went to the Gare de Lyon. She takes us by the arm, Stéphane and me. She is between us, clinging to us for all eternity, or so it seems.

Which of the two of us will draw the child from between her thighs and give it to her, as childlike and virginal as she is herself?

I write: "Checkerboard table. Solid exotic wood from South America, top stained and finished with nitro-cellulose varnish."

Glance out the open window. And that's it for my peace of mind. Just long enough to gaze at a tree in the courtyard. I envy that tree, envy its fullness as a tree, utterly wrapped up in its branches and its leaves, shivering in the light wind. Whereas I am reduced to the most infinitesimal part of myself, typing nonsense for a mail-order catalogue.

A hundred times in a row I write "nitrocellulose." To calm myself. The clicking of my typewriter bears me up and carries me away. Is this any way to live?

Again I glance out the window above my typewriter. The tree in the courtyard is standing there, tranquil. I take a breath. The tree and myself, both perfectly calm.

Suddenly I spy her coming along the paving stones, between flower-beds that aren't yet in bloom. Have heard nothing from her for several days now.

She sits on my bed, winded.

"Too many stairs, Édouard dear. It's too much. Too much."

The same pink dress, more and more shabby. She apologizes, her voice barely audible, assures me none of her clothes fit now except for this pink dress her grandmother gave her a long time ago.

She comes very close to me, says into my ear:

"Stéphane promised me he'd put this dress in the washing machine when he goes to his mother's, and iron it himself."

She appears very pleased with herself and with Stéphane, whereas I become furious with her and Stéphane both.

Delphine pursues her thinking:

"Patrick and the Fat Lady: their marriage won't last long, I don't think. He promised to phone me."

She settles in among the cushions. Begins to recount, speaking to no one in particular, her eyes focused on the open window as if, through the grey day, she sees images that stand out powerfully before her.

"You dumped me at the Gare de Lyon, you and Stéphane, like a package to be delivered. The huge station, the crowds going every which way, people, people everywhere, breathing in my face, bumping my belly as they pass me, my child cries, I hear him crying inside me, I'm afraid for my crying child, afraid for myself lost in a station, Patrick arrives with his suitcases full of flies and fish hooks, just one change of clothes, his razor and aftershave in a toilet-case, right away she wraps him in her great big arms, hides him from me with her broad shoulders, any more and she'll have him on her lap, her fat thighs, her enormous knees, and there will be nothing for me to do but die with my child, who is crying and crying."

Delphine comes so close to me that I can see a little green vein on her temple. She speaks into my ear again:

"All the money is hers, the Fat Lady's — the Paris apartment, the house on Ile de Ré. Everything. Everything. All he has is suitcases filled with sparkling flies and deadly fish hooks, his brown velvet eyes, and his soft, hesitant voice, that knocks me off my feet."

I pick up the sheets of paper scattered over my table. I make piles of them and clip them together. Make a pretence of being very busy. Soon nothing is perceptible in the room but Delphine's voice, uniform, unwavering, too clear. She goes on talking, like someone recalling how she's spent the day before she falls asleep.

"The apartment all sparkling white like a bathtub, the matte white marble fireplace, the fire in the fireplace like the red tip of a lit cigarette against all the white everywhere else in the apartment, the white rug curly as a sheep, a kind of white city all around the living room, with corridors like streets and doors shut like the doors of houses. So magnificent you could die. Patrick inside it like a prince, resting after making his rounds all over the world with his flies and fish hooks. He's earned his apartment on the Trocadéro. And she's there talking to him and calling him 'darling.' If she only knew why I'm so big. . . . And she's invited me for dinner, with lighted candles on the blue tablecloth, a beautiful deep blue against all the white. So gorgeous you could die. The gleaming silverware heavy, very heavy, and glasses that sing under your fingertip, three for each person, a big one and two smaller ones, for drinking different wines, and even water if you want. She's the one who invited me. She had no choice but to be there with him to welcome me. Very polite. Asked me about the baby in my belly. Pretended to know about the backaches, the nausea and all that. Finally asked with seeming kindness: 'When are you due?' All the old questions that old women ask young ones who are swollen like balloons and filled with future. You could see she was polite and well brought up. He must have had to teach her. She'd certainly seen me at the station, waiting for Patrick. She was waiting for him too. The two of us waiting for Patrick. And he pulled in on the train like a prince who travels with suitcases filled with fish hooks and flies. When I turned up for dinner they kissed me, both of them, the way you kiss a well-behaved child. When we were all alone in the living room, with her in the kitchen making coffee, he came up to me, looking like a bereaved man who does what he must to look bereaved, but who deep down is waiting for this difficult moment of sorrow and boredom to be over. He spoke very softly. His brow was knit behind the round lenses of his glasses. He said: 'Be nice, be patient, it will all work out. Give me time . . .' Then he added very quickly, as she was coming in with the coffee: 'I'll call you as soon as I can . . .'"

Delphine sits across from me. Rests her elbows on the table. In a voice that is suddenly close and familiar, she repeats her same little litany, which she's no doubt been repeating time and again throughout her pregnancy:

"It can't go on. Patrick and the Fat Lady married to each other. Patrick's real wife is me. They'll have to face up to it."

Very quickly she goes back to her daydreams, right under my nose, as if I weren't there.

"The apartment — all white and vast, like a white city, a private apartment so luxurious you could die . . ."

Delphine is startled again. Her sharp clear voice. She is looking at me. Two pale sparks come into her eyes, cross the table, and flash in my face.

"And now, Édouard dear, I'm staying in a small hotel, a

very old one on a very old little street, Rue Gît-le-Coeur it's called. A tiny little heart that lies there. At night I can hear that old little heart as it beats within the walls. It keeps me awake."

Stéphane has arrived, all out of breath. He claims that Delphine's ears are too sensitive for her to sleep all alone in a residence so old, so given over to the strange sounds of an ancient time and of the pitch-black night.

After not finding Delphine in her hotel, after running over to my place so he's out of breath, Stéphane seems relieved, as if he was afraid he would never see Delphine again anywhere in the world.

D elphine had very clear ideas about what had to be seen in the city. The fountains, the bridges, and the banks of the Seine attracted her particularly. Whether it was the traffic circle on the Champs-Élysées, the Pont d'Arcole, or the fountain in Place Saint-Michel, we had to wait for Delphine to emerge from her fascination and come back to us.

The great lake and fountains of the Place du Trocadéro. The night, humid and mild. In-line skates. Skateboards. Boys, girls, perched on passing flashes of light. A rumbling hum. The city two steps away. The gushing water. The long liquid flames, white and shuddering. The spray that touches Delphine's hands as she draws near. Again, her stonelike stillness. Her perfect solitude once more.

Nine p.m. at the Place du Trocadéro. A girl and two boys at a table on the terrace of a café they can't afford.

Here she is accepting the cake Stéphane offers her. Didn't see Stéphane order the cake. Didn't see the waiter take the order. Sudden laughter on Delphine's face, where warmth and vivacity have returned. She's laughing because she likes cake, and because she feels she has to laugh to say so. She speaks with her mouth full.

"You can see Patrick's embarrassed to go out with me because of my condition. He bought me a big loose coat that goes down to my heels. He wrapped me up in it. Asked me to wear it all the time when we're together, even when the weather is warm. I don't wear it if he's not there. But when he takes me out, like yesterday when we went to the movies, I keep it on all the time. Even at the restaurant after the movie. I'm suffocating from the heat. But I do what he wants. While I wait for us to get married. He's always asking me to be patient."

Stéphane says:

"The bastard! The bastard!"

Delphine doesn't hear a word Stéphane says. She goes on with her story.

"Once, at the hotel after the restaurant, he didn't want to make love. For fear of squashing the baby. Wouldn't even kiss me. But we could talk with no one else around. I made a scene. He started quivering like a little puppy. To calm me down, he promised he'd tell his wife everything. And he will. He'll tell her and he'll marry me. He has to, after all. I'm pregnant."

She rests her elbows on the table, lets her tea get cold. Loses sight of us, of Stéphane and me, like small figures becoming smaller and smaller as you move off in a boat and little by little the shoreline disappears.

Again her ventriloquist's voice, remote and subdued:

"I think he's very bored in his wife's lovely apartment. A kept man, that's what Patrick Chemin is. His white leather easy chair. I'm sure he's sitting in his white leather easy chair. Looking preoccupied, he sips the coffee the Fat Lady serves him. He'll have plenty of time tomorrow to complain about the coffee keeping him awake."

Stéphane says again:

"The bastard! The bastard!"

I too intervene. I take Delphine's wrist, I squeeze it in my fingers very hard, I shake her arm all the way to the shoulder to make her face me, alive, to make her look at me and talk to me. Her transparent skin. Her green veins visible on her too-white skin, all down the length of her arm.

"Get out, for Christ's sake! Get out girl, before it's too late. You can't stay in limbo like this. Forget about Patrick Chemin and go home."

She looks at me, alarmed. Rubs her wrist as if we'd handcuffed her.

She says:

"You're nasty, Édouard dear. Patrick is a good man. He's the first one I saw on the road, in his old Ford that was falling to pieces, jolting and clattering over the bumps. He picked me up right away, when I'd been racing down the road since morning, the swaying of my grandmother's rocking chair in my ears, my grandmother dead beside her chair, a sudden death, fallen from a rocking chair that went on rocking as if nothing had happened, an evil chair that did it on purpose, the wind that joins in and carries the swaying and breathing of death down the road and far away, that breathing and swaying on the back of my neck as I run, the scent of fields for as far as the eye can see on either side of the road, mixed with the breathing of the wind and of death, the scent of daisies, buttercups, vetch, yarrow that you start to smell in the fields on either side of the road, and even the grass along the ditches, salted with dust, is perfumed by the wind and the breathing of death, and me, I've been running down the road since morning, scented by the fields and by death on the back of my neck, and Patrick drives up in his old car, his suitcases full of flies and fish hooks, and he takes me in, it's the first car I've come across since morning, since the breathing of death on the back of my neck, and I run away, I run till I'm out of breath, the swaying of the rocking chair in my ears, death on the back of my neck, and he is the first one — Patrick Chemin, fishing tackle sales rep — he's the one I have to marry, he's the first, it's an obligation I have."

Stéphane leans towards her as she strays from the point, no doubt hoping to bring her back to us by means of cakes and tea. He calls out:

"Waiter!"

I think, and my chest swells at the thought: she followed the first person who came along, like a baby goose. A phenomenon of her pregnancy, most likely. With Patrick now, and it's for life. Pointless to insist. It could just as well have been me or Stéphane. But it was Patrick. The first person who came along. To replace the grandmother. A question of time and place. Of country. Chance in all its necessity.

Can it be that I'm no longer a man? I just have to do what a man does with a woman. Take her as a man takes a woman. Remove her from her repetitive childhood without delay. Right here, maybe, though it's a busy place, with cars, and blind, deaf people jostling one another while they wait for the 63 bus. Ophelia, Iphigenia, Antigone, and some other diaphanous creatures, doomed to an early death. I'd open her belly, in keeping with male custom, that humped belly of hers, and I'd draw out the little occupant cowering in there. I'd save her from the affliction of being an unwed mother — and crazy on top of it. But I'm not up to that, I don't even deserve to lick her ear in my dreams. And what's the good of losing myself in my savage ruminations? I'm bored to death here between Delphine and Stéphane. I wish I were somewhere else, someplace I'd be alone again.

Still, I miss nothing of what Stéphane and Delphine say or do as they huddle with me around a little table covered with cake crumbs and dirty cups.

Stéphane has just laid his big pale hand with its knotted knuckles over Delphine's little hand, which has wandered onto the table.

"Don't touch me, Stéphane. Your hands are damp, and that gives me goose pimples."

This remark slipped out, but she neither moves nor takes her hand away. No sign on her face of either speech or anger. Delphine sits there motionless, exposed to all and sundry, without modesty or hope.

Stéphane hides his big offended hand in his pocket. He hastens to offer a chocolate eclair to Delphine, who is smiling vaguely.

I go home alone, walking along the quays. The Seine gleams in the night, brighter than it is by daylight. The echo of my footsteps follows me like a noisy shadow, rapid and rhythmical.

F or three weeks we didn't see Delphine or hear of her. As if she were no longer in Paris. She didn't show up at my place or at Stéphane's. She didn't slip in between the tables with her big belly to join us at a café or restaurant. No one spotted her sitting on the stone with the Saint-Sulpice fountain at her back.

Stéphane even wondered if Delphine might be giving birth all by herself in some private clinic, like a cat who goes into hiding to have her kittens.

And then one fine day she rang the bell and walked right into my place, not waiting for me to open the door. She plunked herself down on the rug, in the middle of the room. She lifted her faded pink dress and undid the leather belt she wore against the skin of her waist. She opened her pouch and flung a shower of coins and bills around her. Then her nimble little bird-claws picked everything up, as if thieves were pursuing them. She made piles of coins and bills on the rug. She gazed at what was left of the inheritance from her grandmother, she counted it, and she was desolate.

"I'm ruined. Ruined. All those trains. All those trains. Nice,

Toulouse, Poitiers, Brussels, La Rochelle. The money slips away, along with the trains and hotels. And Patrick, who pretends not to recognize me in the stations and hotels. Who goes marching across hotel lobbies. His long legs like scissors cutting, kicking through the air. Who pretends not to see me, walking fast so he'll lose me in the crowd of travellers. Who's always surprised by my appearance, like a wild animal chased by a sudden storm. Carrying his big suitcases, full of fish hooks and flies, at arm's length. While I have all my belongings on my back, and my inheritance tied around my waist. I was like a lost soul in drafty train stations filled with people weighed down like movers. Despite their haste and their burdens, the air of insult written on their faces, I'm sure all those people who were leaving were judging me on the way by, condemning me as a slut because of my belly and my dress that's too short in front and hangs down in the back."

She is loudly indignant; she curls up and lies on the rug, protecting her belly with her hands. Says she hasn't slept for days and her legs are very cold. I carry her to the bed and cover her with the duvet. A moment later and Delphine goes on talking, as if she's telling herself a story before she goes to sleep.

The story is all about spending long hours in the waiting rooms of strange railway stations, about how hard it is for a pregnant woman to stand up for so long, about her fear of falling and being trampled by travellers.

Delphine suddenly throws off the duvet. She sits on the edge of the bed.

"Good thing I swiped Patrick's diary from his coat pocket last time we were together in Paris, in a sleazy hotel hidden away on the second floor of a fancy restaurant on the quays. I learned it by heart, the way you learn your lesson before you leave for school. I just had to go wherever Patrick was going with his heavy suitcases. To surprise him. To see and be seen by him. Without really wanting to. Or deciding to. Only a diary in my head that I had to follow to the letter to fulfil my need to be with him. A sort of obligation, stronger than everything else. A tremendous stubbornness. I followed him from station to station, from train to train, from town to town, from hotel to hotel. Always, I was there waiting, and he thought he was going crazy. And I thought I was going crazy. Always, he was surrounded by people he knew. They mustn't see us together. Pretend not to know each other in stations and hotels. Me with my loose coat down to my heels. Him with his suitcases, his doe eyes constantly on the lookout in case someone saw him with me. Around three a.m., when no one was there to catch him, an adulterer, in the hallway, he'd come to me, all excited, in his stocking feet on the hall carpet. He worried about the baby and he said that one day he'd have to marry me. All the time he was talking, he kept looking at the time on his wrist. Before he left I'd always create a little scene, and he would too, quietly, not letting himself be too angry for fear someone would hear him in the silence of the night hanging heavily over the hotel."

Alone within herself, no longer facing me as I listen, Delphine recounts her own life, never tiring of it. I let my pen fall to the floor. The blue ink makes a tiny dark stain on the blue carpet. As if it were merely the shadow of the fallen pen.

Delphine is shivering on the bed. I heat water for tea. I ask if she's seen a doctor since she's been in Paris.

Delphine's teeth chatter against the bowl of tea. She looks at me, outraged. Says I mustn't mention doctors to her, ever, or she'll throw herself in the Seine.

High summer over the city. The light on all sides is white, dry, blinding. The shade gnawed away in all its nooks and crannies. The stone radiates, dry as crumbling chalk. White dust. Sweltering heat. Pollution. Sheltered from sweat and tears, Delphine resembles a little fish that's been salted dry. Her baby curls up inside her and is silent.

She casts no shadow in the strong sunlight that devours her. Only the fleeting shadow of her big belly against a wall when she goes into town, pushing her belly before her like a steep rock. Under these conditions — extreme weight in her centre and a ravenous beast deep in her entrails — she raises frail, green-veined arms to the sky. Yells. Demands justice. Absolute justice that would depend only on her own law, Delphine's law, an ideal law, despite the common sense and notions of justice held by married women and timorous men. With the railway timetable carefully memorized, and Patrick Chemin's schedule at her fingertips, she tracks him down and runs into him in out-of-town hotels located near the train station, just long enough for them to exchange the resentment they both feel, to whisper it in strange bedrooms, stopping themselves from bursting out, the way people hold back their cries when making love, because of the neighbours.

"I forbid you to follow me around like my shadow. If anyone sees us together I'll be ruined. You're in my way. I can't stand you. I'll see you in Paris, as usual."

"I have to be where you are. To shame you. So you can see me as I am, in a terrible state. So you can learn me by heart and never forget me."

Could anyone but her do that better than she does, and plead her case? Could anyone proclaim louder than her the wrong that was done to her when she was numb with horror after her grandmother's death, and death has been hard on her heels long enough that the cold breath on her neck has stopped, and the cold wind at her back, and the funereal scent of late-summer flowers, usually unscented, that had begun to smell strong like graveyard flowers, and he was inside the heat of the world, he took her inside his own heat, which was the radiant, penetrating heat of the world. The road was deserted, like a bare hand separated from its arm and shoulder, all alone in the naked air. He arrived in the bareness of the road where she'd been running since morning, her elbows close to her body, the wind on her neck like an icy knife. His clattering car, his fishing tackle in the black suitcases on the back seat. He had her get in the car beside him, choking, nearly dead from having run so far. He gave her a big white handkerchief. Told her to wipe her eyes and blow her nose. She does everything he tells her to do. He takes charge of her. He consoles her. He repeats, "Such a terrible affliction," and he cries too. She says she has nobody now. She clings to him like a lost cat. It is autumn everywhere along the flat road where he picked her up, suffocating. They drive over the mountain, where the maple trees blaze here and there against the blackish green of the spruce and the gold of the birches. A glimmer, like light seen through stained glass, enters the clamorous little car when he offers her candy. For the first time she sees his doe eyes with their long black lashes against his pale cheek. She starts to cry again, repeats that she's alone in the world. He squeezes her fingers hard enough to make her cry. A little more and he'll claim that he's all alone too. Which would be true in a way, though he has recently married. It doesn't make sense to say he's all alone, even if he secretly feels he is. With his wife or without her, moreover. An irreparable solitude, no doubt. This man has never in his life consoled someone else, always being the most unhappy. He is elated and comforted to be able to do so with Delphine. To deliver her from tears and from the suffocation of tears. He desires this for the first time — the power of the stronger in the face of the weaker. He melts with gratitude. Feels infinite pity. He drapes his jacket over Delphine's shoulders. Now that she has stopped crying, she's freezing from head to toe as if it were winter.

They pull into town around six p.m., in the little dark green car that bounces and rattles.

All that happened in Delphine's country, well before Patrick's return to France, where that woman was waiting for him — she who remained, in his most deeply hidden thoughts, his wife and sovereign for all eternity.

Stéphane insisted on going with Delphine to the Gare Montparnasse. She departed for Nantes without seeing Stéphane, as she was busy having her ticket punched and trying to locate her railway car on the platform.

He comes to my place as soon as he can get away from the record store where he works. He's waiting for Delphine. Though he appears to be as drained of all passion as a little dead fish on a plate. His blank eyes gaze at me, unseeing.

Delphine has come back sooner than expected. She assures me that she'll never see Patrick Chemin again as long as she lives, that she'd rather die.

She pats her belly and seems close to giving birth. She creases her eyes in her little freckled face, makes an effort to see the shadows breathing in my paper-littered studio. She even declares that she can discern very clearly, directly ahead of her, the troubled face of Patrick Chemin. This man hasn't been doing at all well since Delphine cursed him in Nantes.

"He's very pale and he's sweating bullets. His wife wipes

his forehead with a Kleenex. She fixes him a soothing drink. Her movements are those of a giant who is doing her best to care for a normal-sized human being. Though his legs are too long. The tiny torso of a sick child. Narrow shoulders. No one sees him more clearly than I do, with his flaws and his good points. His incomparable eyes. He has the brown velvet eyes of a doe. His long, long lashes cast a shadow on his cheek. I've never looked at anyone the way I look at him. I carved his name on my heart with a sharp little knife, all the letters of his name in capitals. All the features of his face in large characters. His legs like scissor blades. The stupid look on his face when I told him he'd have to choose between his wife and me. The fat old lady or me — young and full to bursting with life. I have double everything: kidneys, liver, heart, arms, legs, sex. I'm a double-yolked egg. Carefully hidden behind my navel there's a living beast that swells and grows from hour to hour, that eats me and drinks me, that presses on my bladder with all its weight, sucking its thumb and making itself comfortable as if it were at home."

She looks us in the eye, Stéphane and me. Her laughter tumbles from her like a shower of hail.

"Would you like to know, my little papas, exactly what Patrick Chemin said to make me curse him in Nantes? 'I'll never marry you. I'm tied to another woman in spite of myself, by a powerful force that comes from her alone, that binds us to each other until death . . .' I told him that real life was on my side, and that, if he didn't marry me, he'd soon be dead and buried, rotten from remorse and sin."

From laughter Delphine moves on to tears. Then laughs again. She is shaken by laughter interrupted by sobs.

"The worst part was when he asked me to forgive him and he wanted to put his ear against my belly and listen to my child's heart, like a doctor. I couldn't bear having him so close to the frantic beating of my life, so I scratched him on the cheek. Then I jumped to my feet in the hotel room. I buttoned my long coat up to the neck and I left, all alone, in the middle of the night. The wait till morning in the empty railway station at Nantes was the longest of all the times I've waited in stations and on platforms. But I'll never again go anywhere to see him and touch him, to be seen and touched by him. Lovers who see each other and touch each other in the madness of being in love. I think I'm going to give birth right away, at your place, Édouard dear. I've been looking so long for a quiet, comfortable nest . . ."

Threat and counter-threat. At once I talked to Delphine about a doctor, a hospital. In one leap she was at the door. Raced down the stairs. We could hear her shouting from one floor to the next:

"I'll give birth the way I want, when I want, where I want. It's nobody's business but mine."

Leaning on the windowsill, I see her hurry across the courtyard and disappear under the porch, with Stéphane following and shouting at her.

He caught up with her at the corner of Rue de Rennes, as she was turning onto Rue Cassette, just as school was letting out. They talked together, surrounded by the crowd of children, breathless from running.

"Do you want to marry me?"

He was panting so hard that the words broke off in his throat. She kissed his cheek to thank him. For a moment his hurried breath and hers were mingled.

"No, Stéphane, no, I can't."

He was wrong to insist, because Delphine's anger came rushing back. She ran away again, shouting insults at Patrick and at Stéphane, who fed her anger because he was within her reach just then. She cried:

"No, Stéphane, no, Patrick Chemin is the one I want. And anyway your hands are damp, poor Stéphane, I don't want you to touch me!"

Stéphane let her dash away, bumping into the tables and chairs lined up on the sidewalk outside the corner café. Very quickly he lost sight of her.

We heard nothing more about Delphine for several days. Her baggage stayed on the floor of her hotel room, and her bed wasn't slept in.

Stéphane told me all about it, and I pointed out to him that the girl was crazy.

W hat can be done for Delphine who has disappeared? Her pregnancy. Her madness. Her threadbare cotton dress. The inheritance from her grandmother, which is dwindling visibly. The man who made her pregnant. His refusal to marry her. Stéphane and I have decided to adopt Delphine and her child. We've bought a layette, baby clothes, and maternity clothes in a shop that caters to pregnant woman. We've started looking for her in the city.

No doubt it's pointless to shake the city in every direction, like a rug, in the hope of finding Delphine. Streets, squares, alleys, cafés, railway stations — ah yes, especially the stations. She cannot be found.

Stéphane says her name to anyone who will listen.

"Her name is Delphine. Have you seen her? She's a pregnant girl who . . ."

Lost from the outset, like a puppy found in a garbage can — wandering since the dawn of this world in some vague country we can only imagine — Delphine well and truly cannot be found. The two of us, Stéphane and I, can trace her appalling little life no farther back than a grandmother and a rocking chair that moves back and forth on a wooden verandah. Delphine says her grandmother no longer has milk or periods. That reassures her. The old woman cannot release some noisy baby from her dry womb, from under her pulled-up skirts. She won't insult her granddaughter by replacing her with another brat. An only child forever, she breathes and settles herself in her grandmother's lap, against the big, dry, warm breasts. Even though she is ten years old. Childhood rediscovered seems eternal. But now things are falling apart and the whisper of death can be heard. That bitter whisper cannot be the wind, though the rocking chair continues to move back and forth after the grandmother has fallen dead to the ground. Such swaying back and forth in her ears, and the road before her so she can run away until she's out of breath. And now, on this side of the Atlantic, it's beginning again. Once again Delphine is running away, with death at her heels, or so she thinks.

The Fat Lady is here before me. Now I can see her up close. The texture of her skin, the curl of her hair, the breadth of her hips, the blaze of her anger, the passage of words on her red lips, her carnivorous teeth. I can hear her breathe.

Having emerged from Delphine's story as if by magic, the Fat Lady is at my place. She is sitting on my bed and crossing her legs. But how can this be?

She dragged a sheepish Patrick Chemin to Rue Gît-le-Coeur in the hope of finding Delphine and taking the child from her. With Delphine gone, the hotel-keeper insists that someone get rid of her baggage.

At that very point in the conversation with the hotel-keeper, about the baggage, Stéphane turned up, and the three of them met and recognized one another, making Delphine's world virtually complete. All that remained was for me to join them and to join in their commitment to find Delphine.

All Patrick does is plead that we go to the railway stations and look for Delphine there.

Her fury paces the narrow room. Her long strides. Her endless legs. My back is to the wall. Shut away with her inside her rage and her insults. I, with my restricted life, my limited desires, I am suffocating in here with her, between the table and the bed.

She strides back and forth. She has the ceiling at her head, the walls at her fingertips, she need only reach out her arms. Now she is circling me, glaring, dancing. Her short linen jacket spins around with every step. Her odour is on me. She speaks into my face.

"Patrick has told me everything about that little girl. He was trembling from head to toe. He looked like a stuffed toy being shaken."

Shall I take advantage of her anger, rub myself against it like a match, and blaze in turn from a strong and violent life?

But look at her now, outrageously mild and asking for something to eat and drink.

I offer her bread and cheese. I set a half-full bottle on the table.

I watch her eat and drink, standing across from her, arms hanging by my sides but somehow awkward, as if I were holding a hat in my right hand and a bouquet of flowers in my left, the better to salute her rapacity — or perhaps this fury of hers, that is soothed as she eats and drinks.

"I'm very greedy, and my greed will be the death of me. I like *choucroute*, bacon omelets, good ripe Camembert, and my dear little husband — oh God, how dear he is, my dear, dear, dear husband who has cheated on me . . ."

Her deafening laughter makes the windows rattle.

Not a drop left in the bottle, not a crumb left on the plate.

She gets up from the table, stretches and yawns, her mouth

wide open as if she wants to swallow everything around her — invisible pollen suspended in the motionless air, every living particle eddying within my walls, and me, standing there before her like an edible insect.

Something infinite in her arms and thighs. The giantess moves like a panther in a cage.

"I have to adopt that child. He's half mine as it is, since Patrick is the father. I'm ravenous, and everything I lust after is already mine."

She has started to smoke. She blows smoke-rings big enough for me to step through, like a circus act, wearing all my clothes and with my big boots on my feet.

This creature is beautiful and terrifying. Her name is Marianne Chemin.

The waiting room, Gare Saint-Lazare, seven p.m.

Marianne is the first to recognize her, having looked for her more zealously than anyone else. The crowd walks by, going in every direction, dazing her and jostling her. Now she has neither grace nor beauty. Her dress is a rag on her skin. Her head is as empty as a black hole. You can see beads of sweat on her forehead.

From very far away, Marianne has seen the pink stain of Delphine's dress as she stands pinned against the wall. She moves towards her, picks her out, holds her. With her head thrown back and her hands on her belly, Delphine is without defences or vivacity. She is ripe like a fruit that is past its prime, one that holds within it another fruit that is practically overripe and ready to fall to the ground.

Once they're in the taxi on their way to the Hôtel-Dieu hospital, amid countless cars driving along in the sunlight, the two women are so close to one another on the back seat that Marianne can feel Delphine's contractions through her own sterile body, resonating in her like waves against a seawall. And if Delphine turns around, she can feel

Marianne's gaze fixed on her like the black eye of a squirrel preparing to break a nut to get at its kernel. *I want that child and I'll have it*, thinks Marianne.

Delphine is moaning continuously now. She has arrived at the peak of her lie and of her little drama.

The over-abundant life she thought she possessed has been taken from her. Her imposture has been found out and she is dumbfounded.

Her cries through the walls of the Hôtel-Dieu.

Marianne, Patrick, Stéphane, and I confined to the waiting room. Cries everywhere, all around us. What goes on here is like the earth forced open so new blood will come.

Patrick never looks up from the tiles at his feet. We can see the top of his head, his thinning hair. You'd think that his misfortune was hidden down there, between two tiles, that if he bent down he'd be able to rip it out like a weed.

Briefly he raises his head, and I observe the eyes that Delphine praised so highly. Excessively gentle, with an other-worldly velvet smoothness, Patrick Chemin's eyes express what he will never say to Delphine. Tender compassion is lost between his eyelashes. At the peak of disaster. Doesn't know whom to ask for forgiveness. Delphine or Marianne? Wants above all to be rocked and consoled.

The midwife approaches us. Tells us that the girl was full of air, like a wineskin. She laughs reluctantly, too surprised to poke fun openly.

"False pregnancy! Did you ever hear the like, I ask you? A unique case in the annals of the Hôtel-Dieu."

More exhausted than if it had all been real, a cry caught in her throat, Delphine finally dozed off long after she was placed in a hospital bed, an injection in the crook of her arm.

As she walks past the nursery, Marianne carefully studies the newborns behind the glass, as if she were looking through the impassable waters of birth. Her long hand, with its gleaming wedding band, raps against the glass wall.

S he is silent on her hospital bed. Utterly mute. Still as a stone. Flat as a sole. A dead fish. Nothing is happening any more, in her belly or in her heart. She has been burst open. Stripped of her heaviness. Now she is reduced to her empty form. Narrow and thin. The imaginary fruit has been tossed into the naked air, mingled with the nudity of the air, sucked in by the naked air, reduced to dust and powder, spread, impalpable, through the great void above the roof-tops, disappearing on the horizon like the ashes of the dead, vanished over the sea.

A beautiful summer. Paid holidays. Vacations planned since last year. The sea. The mountains. The countryside. Children. Parents. Grandparents. Evanescent loves appearing on the horizon. They all go away. Nearly everyone. Pretend they know nothing of Delphine's extravagant dream that has been swallowed up by the chalky air of a summer day.

They have not seen her thinness, the sheet that her flat little bones barely lift as she lies tidily on the hospital bed. They have taken advantage of her absolute silence and her refusal to see anyone at all to leave on vacation as usual.

Marianne has taken Patrick to Ile de Ré, to the big house that has been hers since her parents' death. Ashamed as though he himself had given birth to a chimera, Patrick has sworn that never again will he be taken in.

I brought flowers to her in the hospital. She closed her eyes so as not to see them. Pinched her nose so as not to smell them. Her hand came away with difficulty from her chest, where it had been fixed like the dead hand of a martyred woman, palm open over her heart, in old paintings. She gestured for the flowers and their odour to be taken away, and went back to sleep, the sleep of the dead.

Stéphane no longer listens to music — or if he does try to listen to some kind of music he used to like before he knew Delphine, his pale face looks drawn, as if he were hearing discordant notes ringing in his ears.

After the hospital discharged her, we checked out the classified ads in Le Figaro.

"'Villa Anthelme. 17th arrondissement. Métro Wagram. Room and board.'"

Stéphane and I went there, accompanying a sleepwalker who mustn't be wakened for fear she might throw herself under the first car that came along.

The narrow sofa was covered with a rough fabric in a dark blue that was nearly black. The double window open to the stifling summer didn't stop the musty smell from tickling our noses.

Delphine has been leaning out the window into the sticky heat, looking at the long inner courtyard with its paving stones pried partially loose, and she declares that this is fine, that no one will dare cross the bumpy courtyard to come and disturb her for fear of spraining an ankle.

She turns down the blue blanket. Sees that the sheets are clean. Gets into bed fully dressed. Turning to face the wall, she asks us to let her sleep. While Stéphane and I are still there looking at her, Delphine sinks into sleep, tired from the move by taxi and from life in general.

Stéphane says that he loves Delphine more than his mother, that it's terrible, and that Delphine doesn't love him at all.

The telegram arrived almost immediately after Stéphane's declaration: "Mother sick. Asks son to come. A neighbour."

Stéphane took the train for Meudon the next morning. He wouldn't come back to Paris till after Delphine's death.

I believe I can picture Stéphane comfortably ensconced in a seat on the train, heading for Meudon, travelling full speed through the countryside, not so much as moving his little finger, inert and taken in charge by one of the powers of this world. I know, however, that his musician's soul distinctly hears Delphine's little voice, lilting and insidious, amid the deafening clatter of the wheels along the rails.

As for Stéphane's mother, whether she's sick or not, I have no precise idea of her, having barely seen her, a dark widow, one night in her house at Meudon. With Stéphane on his way to her, it's a little as if he were sinking gradually into the opacity of the earth.

The air is like oil. A heat wave in all its splendour. My solitude restored. Quick errands between two paragraphs. Stairways rushed down, then right up again, on the double. Baguette. Coffee. Ham sandwich with butter. Cheap red wine. Cheese. Summer berries. I barely exist and I write paragraphs. I abandon Stéphane's loves and plunge into maxi-furnishings for mini-salaries. All's well that ends well.

The world is in order. I work. Delphine sleeps at the Villa Anthelme. Stéphane is sinking into the maternal shadows before our eyes. Fear the mystery of the other like my own forbidden memory.

I'm at home, revelling in the stuffy air, when Delphine comes bursting in, shining from head to foot as if she's just out of the water. Her maternity dress, brightly coloured and unwrinkled, hangs loosely over her tiny body. Her high cheekbones seem freshly polished.

"See how nicely I'm dressed, Édouard dear? Everything's new. The dress, the shoes, all of it, all of it. I just had to choose from the trousseau you and Stéphane bought me. Down the toilet with my pink dress and the lump that was inside it. I'll never see Patrick Chemin again. Take a good look at me — alone, thin, and flawless! A genuine marvel!"

She spins around. Her oversized dress is like a swollen lampshade around her. Her crepe-soled shoes squeak on the carpet. Her long hair flies over her face and down her back.

"I came to tell you about the Villa Anthelme. Would you like to hear what goes on there?"

She is here, at my place, in a room littered with papers and catalogues, all vibrant with laughter and with the secrets of the Villa Anthelme.

"At first I thought no one was there. Except the maid, who seemed to be the real mistress of the house. It suited me that there was no one in the house except for the maid and me. Silence everywhere, as dense as water. She brings my food on a tray. I don't eat. I pretend to be always asleep. The silence from me is added to the silence of the house. Outside, it's summer. I rage and I cry in my bed against the wall. The maid calls me Little Misery. There's a tiny wash-basin with an S-shaped pipe. I wash my hair in it. I plug in my hair dryer. Immediately, there's a rustle of slippers everywhere, coming awake in the house. Going up and down the stairs. Brushing against my door. Feet scuffling everywhere. Buzzing like a swarm of flies in the dark.

"'Somebody's blown the fuses!'

"The answer echoes back:

"'Who blew the fuses?'

"I huddle in my bed. The shattered silence of the house is intolerable. The silence ought to be glued back together so I can hide deep inside it again. I don't want anyone to see me. I pull the sheet over my face. There's a knock at my door. I put my hands over my ears. The maid bursts into my room. She unplugs the hair dryer. Says it's forbidden. She's very angry. My eyes are wide open at the maid's anger. I see her thick lips quivering with anger. Now there are old people all over the landing, craning their necks to look through the open door into my room. The old people have emerged from their holes like rats. I hide in my bed as best I can. I'm so afraid that all at once I get my voice back. I scream:

"'Shut the door!'

"Once the door has been shut and the maid has gone, I cry my eyes out, I can't stop, till evening. It's a change from the silence that's been stifling me for days. Around eight o'clock the maid comes to see me with bread and ham on a plate. She says:

"'You're carrying on too much, Little Misery. Now stop it. Your pillow's soaking wet.'

"She wipes my face with the hem of her white-flowered red dress.

"Her name is Farida. She's the real mistress of the Villa Anthelme. The old people just have to behave themselves. She scolds them one by one, each in turn, and she runs everything like a real queen."

Delphine is talking faster and faster. She can't get the words out quickly enough. The tempo of her speech has been restored to her a hundredfold. After a very long silence she really gets going.

"If you only knew, Édouard dear, the things that go on at the Villa Anthelme."

She delights at the rest of her account in advance, as if it were an avalanche of words preparing to tumble down.

The heat seeps in through the closed shutters. Delphine looks out between the slats at the courtyard baking in the sun. She comes back to me.

"I wanted to take a bath before I came to see you. Soap myself from head to toe. I washed my hair yesterday, but already it's like spun glass. So much accumulated sweat, grime, and tears. I want to erase every sign of my past life. Forget Patrick Chemin. Get a new skin. Into the sea at noon. Start from square one. Never be fat again, or sad. Here I am before you for the first time. Take a good look at me. See how clean and new I am. My imaginary child is in the garbage. As for the bath, Farida told me I could. She assured me that the youngest of the old people bathes on the days his girlfriend comes to visit. The bathroom is big and high like a chapel, and the tub sits on a platform like an altar. Four doors flatten the four corners. No key. The tub as deep as an abyss. The still, hot water Farida has run. The verdigris copper taps. I'm in water up to my chin. My hair in a chignon on top of my head. The delight of all that water. I breathe under water. I blow bubbles. In a little while, a strange rustling comes into the gentle foaming of the bubbles, from the other side of the doors. The old people are spying on me through the keyholes. I hear them breathing and stamping at the four compass points. I get out of the water as fast as the wind, and wrap myself in the huge towel Farida has laid out. The one and only big, white, soft terrycloth towel in the Villa Anthelme. The other towels are the size of a gauze pad, they're scratchy and they don't dry you properly. Farida brings me something to eat and drink. She tucks me in even when I pout against the wall. She scolds me and wipes away my tears. Her big breasts. Her swollen mouth. If she looks away for just a minute, I go back to the street and follow the first person who comes along, dogging his footsteps till he turns to me and takes charge of me."

I point out to Delphine that it would be best if she stayed at the Villa Anthelme as long as she can before she goes back to her country.

"I don't have a country. Get that into your head, Édouard dear. No country at all. Where I come from was my grandmother, only my grandmother, and she's dead."

The beautiful summer is stagnating in the courtyard and above the city, is ripening gently, secretly preparing its decline and its end. I'm reading *Murder on the Orient Express*. I lose my way in the obscure plot. I think I hear a steam engine whistling in the night, while in full daylight, at home on Rue Bonaparte, the muffled sound from the porte-cochère rings out and slowly fades.

It's her. It can't be anyone else. I listen for her footsteps on the stairs. I drop my book. I hear a child's voice calling to me through the door:

"Are you there, Édouard dear? I need to talk to you right now!"

Her hair, plaited into two long braids that pull at her temples, makes her look more offended than usual.

"I'm not hanging around the Villa Anthelme any longer. I'd rather go back to the street."

She stretches out on my bed, slaps her braids against her shoulders like whips. Straightens up and says in a strained voice, urged by I know not what wild wind that presses on her and leaves her breathless:

AM I DISTURBING YOU?

"I have to tell you. Since yesterday, Farida has refused to bring my meals to my room. She flung me into the dining room with the old people. I have to face the old people at the table in the dining room of the Villa Anthelme. My arrival creates a sensation. They all look up. Their gazes all focus on me. They stop chewing when I sit down. They drop their forks and knives to look at me. The silence they cast over me is like black ice. A field of black ice to catch me in, to put me into the same state as them, like poor frozen beasts."

Nervously Delphine undoes her braids. Her hair, set free, corkscrews around her. She brings her hands together, groans in a barely perceptible voice:

"Farida doesn't look after me. She leaves me all by myself. I'd got used to her warmth, the warmth of a living creature. The others give me goose pimples. Their cold hands. The way they roll their eyes — the eyes of a malevolent dead fish. And Farida, who goes from table to table dishing out the meat, rice, or vegetables, the cheese or stewed fruit. She refuses to change Madame Lebeau's plate between the meat and the fruit. With her hands on her hips she declares, so all the people in the dining room, who are listening in silence, can hear:

"'You old owl. Are you the one that washes the dishes?'

"I saw that Farida was as fierce with the poor creatures as an animal tamer swinging his stick inside a cage."

She talks. I listen. The long hours of midsummer, drop by drop. Suddenly she falls silent. Gathers her impressions. Doesn't know how to approach them. Steeps herself in silence again. Silently regains the power of speech. Broods on the insult to Madame Lebeau. Swallows at length. Briskly flips her hair over her shoulders. Decides to say something but doesn't know quite how to go about it. Thinks very hard about Madame Lebeau and how she was insulted by the maid.

"She left the table without picking up her napkin, which had fallen to the floor. She walked right across the dining room, head high, feet awkward in her house slippers. Everyone watching. Everyone listening. It's so rare that anything happens at the Villa Anthelme. We hear Madame Lebeau shuffling up the stairs, step by step, breathless and plaintive. Her door on the second floor slams in the vast silence. We go back to eating, but more slowly, moving food from one cheek to the other, like a child who doesn't want to swallow. For three days, not a sign of Madame Lebeau. Nowhere. Not in the dining room. Not on the stairs. Not in the hallway that leads to the bathroom. By the third day I wondered if she was dead in her room. I knocked on her door. Several times. With a pause between knocks. Eventually she came to the door. Brusque, like some crank. I asked how she was. I observed that she was very much alone. She jumped out of her room. A little grey viper about to bite. She came into my room. My door stayed wide open. Her amazing speed. Her quick little movements that could stagger you, body and soul. She repeated 'alone,' 'alone,' as if she were tearing the word between her teeth, spitting it on the ground, then picking it up to bite it again.

"'Everyone's alone. I'm alone. You're alone. Or maybe you're hiding someone? Under your bed? In your closet?'

"She looks under the bed. She looks in the closet. Shaking like a leaf.

"'You can see there's nobody anywhere.'

"She whispers, like an echo, 'nobody,' and 'anywhere,' breathing very fast, looking deathly tired.

"Then she totters out and double-locks herself inside her own room."

Delphine ends her speech with a great sigh, brings Madame Lebeau's solitude back to herself, is engulfed in it for a moment.

"Once in my life I was more alone than Madame Lebeau, the very worst of all the times in the world, and that was after my grandmother died. And now that Farida has kicked me out, it's starting again."

She is talking in her stranger's voice again, very low, her soul and her heart so far away that I feel I'm hearing her in a dream.

Caught in the act of listening and heeding, I refuse to follow this little girl along the uncertain roads of loss and desolation. For want of anything better to do, I offer her food and drink. I set the table and heat up a pizza.

She eats and drinks warily. Barely sips her wine. Spits the anchovies onto the edge of her plate, the olive pits into the ashtray. She gazes fixedly at me across the table and prepares what she is going to say. Lays down her knife and fork.

"Please, Édouard dear, let me sleep here, only sleep. I've left the Villa Anthelme."

She wants me to be kind and compassionate, while I rage and refuse.

I make her lie down in the bed right against the wall. I, the true master of the bed, stretch out at the other edge. I leave the light on. I look at her. She's pale and thin. She looks at me. I am heavy and dark, with curly hair. When I pull off my shirt, she turns away. I switch off the light. Undress in the dark. Stretch out again. A lock of her hair brushes my shoulder. I lift it off at once. I establish a clear boundary in the very middle of the bed, a kind of no man's land where it's best not to venture. It's not that this girl excites me, but I'm afraid of I know not what sombre power emanating from her small person as she is given over in the darkness to the old demons that torment her.

She is lying there perfectly flat under the sheet, moving neither her head nor her body. Her profile indistinct in the dark. Barely audible words break away from her, move across my cheek like warm mist.

"At the Villa Anthelme there's someone who's hidden, someone more highly placed than Farida, who gives orders to the whole house in secret. Someone authoritarian and sacred stands behind a closed double door with dark mouldings, on the ground floor just next to the front door. She's the one who is really in charge of the Villa Anthelme. When I was walking down the hall this morning, I heard her voice, an old woman's voice, bellow and break. No doubt angry at having played dead for so many days and nights now, she was crying out to make up for the time she'd lost. Farida received her anger, flung by the bucketful. I saw Farida go in like a little girl waiting to be punished. I saw her come out again, all limp in her floral-patterned dress, like a big red and white flower withering and drooping on its stem. Farida saw me — saw that I knew everything, that I'd been standing there in the lobby for several minutes. She couldn't bear no longer being the queen in my eyes. She turned on me. Her eyes were bulging out of her head like shiny marbles, black and white. She cried out in turn:

"'Get out of here, Little Misery! I don't want to see your face any more! Get the hell out!'

"She helped me pack my bags. Her hands were trembling. She threw me out on the street. And she hailed a taxi, waving both arms over her head as if she were calling for help."

What do I do with this girl lying beside me in my bed, like an old wife telling me about her day? I think I'll dream all alone at her side, like a very old husband. She says good night, and she drapes her hair across her face, to hide.

S he pretends to be drinking her café au lait, face buried in her bowl up to the eyes. Confesses that she's not crazy about coffee.

I make her some tea.

Between us, no conversation is possible. She's too sleepy, it seems, to launch into one of her customary long monologues. And I'm too much on my guard again to want to listen to her. I'm annoyed at her for having slept in my bed. I retreat into silence in front of her and wait for her to go away.

A sleepwalker who butters slices of bread and dips them in her tea. Her slow movements nearly coming to a standstill above the plate and bowl. A little more and her knife and her little spoon will fall to the tablecloth, and sleep will make her head droop to her chest. She murmurs that she's very tired.

I tell her that if she wants to stay in Paris, she'll have to look for work. She admits, her lips barely moving, that she's never worked and doesn't know how to do anything.

She closes her eyes, turns very pale, speaks softly —

listening to a voice, it seems, that repeats as an echo in the absolute void of the room.

"My grandmother used to say that I was a poor little thing who hurt all over, and that I needed to rest."

Her blind face comes very close to me above the table. She speaks with her mouth shut. I guess at, rather than hear, what she is saying.

"They stole my child at the Hôtel-Dieu. They told me he was dead. They said I was stark raving mad. How do you expect me to work like everybody else?"

And all at once she brightens up, grave and in full possession of what she sees before her.

"My grandmother spends all Sunday afternoon rocking on the front verandah. On Sunday the rockers of her big, shiny, red straw-bottomed chair go back and forth on the floor of the verandah for hours. I like their smooth sound, it joins the murmur from the fields all around. I can hear that gentle rubbing of wood against wood in my head day and night, in Paris, Nantes, Aix, on Rue Gît-le-Coeur, at the Saint-Sulpice fountain, at the Villa Anthelme. When she died, my grandmother fell out of her rocking chair on the verandah. Not one moan. Not one sigh. Not a single cry for help. She fell like someone who has finished rocking and lets herself drop to the ground. A sound both muffled and light. The wind was blowing so hard that day, the empty chair kept rocking by itself in the wind while my grandmother was lying there dead on the ground. The doctor. The priest. The notary. I did what had to be done. At the house. At the church. At the graveyard. In the notary's office. I went to all the places you have to go to in cases of death, burial, and inheritance. The wind was still blowing. The rocking chair kept moving back and forth by itself in the wind. I couldn't stand that relentless creaking and I set out down the main highway, leaving the house I'd inherited to squatters, and the chair rocking on the verandah. Safe in a small leather pouch that I fastened to my belt was the other part of my inheritance, in coins and bills. Just enough to survive on until someone took care of me again. I walked along the road for hours, over the horizon, I think, and I thought I would die."

Both her face and her body change before my eyes. Here she is in front of me, filled with terror and tears, running away from her grandmother's death on the road. Too much, it's too much. I'm disgusted and I turn my head away. All this girl wants is my tears in return for hers. I will not grant her that complicity. Dry as an old tree against a stone wall, I inform Delphine that she'll have to find another shelter for the coming night. I give her the address of a small hotel in Montparnasse that someone told me about.

É douard dear, do you want to know what's going on in the Rue J.C.? It's a street full of girls swaying on their high heels. Redheads, blondes — they lost their original colour long ago — they blaze in the sun or the rain, among the gaudy neon signs. Starting at four in the afternoon. The tallest one has the red mane of a mad mare hanging all the way down her back. Her gleaming black boots come up to her thighs and they are inlaid with bits of mirrors. We meet on the sidewalk. She's constantly parading back and forth. I'm looking for my hotel. She despises me, she hates me from the first hard, furtive glance. Édouard dear, why did you drop me there in the middle of all those hookers? The hotels are named for flowers: Les Hortensias, Les Glycines, Le Volubilis. Only the Saint-Gildas displays its name, the name of a Breton saint, in phosphorescent letters. That's where you sent me to sleep. I was wide awake all night. The big clock on the wall in my room sounds the quarter-hour and the half-hour with a muffled thud. Beneath my window the red mare paces the sidewalk and hates me along the way, through the closed shutters. I'd rather sleep at your place,

Édouard dear. It's more peaceful. Just sleep. I'm so tired. Ever since I've had my grandmother's death chasing me, and Patrick Chemin, who is rotten. So long, big brother. Till tonight.

Delphine

I found this letter when I came back from a long stroll along the quays. The Seine was flowing slow and grey in the mist, and the edge of the water disappeared into the hazy sky. A wan light rose from the river, as it does when there's snow on the ground and the earth is brighter than the air. It was the beginning of September. The thought of Delphine followed my every step, like a stray cat that twines itself around your legs, that you refuse to look at for fear you'll have to take it in.

I barely have time to read her letter, which she's slipped under the door, when there she is, with her bundle on her back. She says she's tired. She stretches out on my bed and stays there, fully dressed, listening to her weariness. She spies on her motionless body, searching for the deep-seated reasons for her distress.

"'Where does it hurt, sweetheart?' my grandmother would ask."

She repeats that she's tired. I tell her she'll have to get a job like everyone else. She laughs. Gets up abruptly. Swears she doesn't hurt anywhere. I notice how small and white her teeth are.

Delphine is telling her story again, as if she can't stop, regardless of what it may cost her.

"Excused from dishes, housework, cooking, from mending,

from hens and rabbits, by my grandmother, who does everything in my place, I rest. At night I no longer hear the cries of hungry infants piercing my skull. I sleep to my heart's content, day and night. Between naps, I read. A huge fatigue turns up between books, between naps. A black hole to swallow me up. The poets keep me company, and I'm damned along with them, in the books and in my room in the country where I read. I read and I dream about hell and about the scarlet sky at the end of hell, like a bright border of flames. Always, my grandmother comforts me and says sweet things to me, things so comforting and sweet after my huge storms of incomprehensible pain. I hear her empty chair rocking on the empty verandah. I escape from that intolerable rocking by hurrying down the deserted road. My footsteps resound on the asphalt. Tap, tap, tap. A real runaway horse. But smaller. Not so strong. A little clicking of hoofs on the asphalt. A very small runaway horse. Driven onto the road. A very small, panicky clicking along the asphalt. And I'm nearly out of breath, close to dying. The first car stops. The first person appears. His head out the window. His head bent towards me. His gaze, like no other. Let him look at me just once more and I'll be his entirely. Let him recognize me straightaway as his inexpressible soul, let him take me with him right away, to a life that is comforting and sweet. Out of this world. Let him settle me in a safe place filled with incomparable love. An impenetrable place where I'll be safe from terror. There are black suitcases piled on the back seat of his car. He gazes at me with his doe eyes. His long lashes. He is Patrick Chemin. He comes from another land, across the ocean. He sells flies and fish hooks. I have to be picked up right away or I'll drop dead on the hill. Too many kilometres in my body. Haven't eaten. Or drunk. Too much walking down the road. My grandmother's chair keeps swaying in the wind behind me. I go limp and I fold, like cloth. My breathing pounds outside of me. Let me get my breath back. The wet grass where I fall full-length chills me and swallows me up at the same time. I've passed out in the wet grass. He carries me to his car, which smells of beer and smoke. Puts a compress on my forehead. Takes me to town."

She is alone before me, as I am alone before her. She extracts her life from between her ribs, a little at a time. I respond with the brutality of the deaf, who hear nothing and who measure neither voice nor speech.

"You always talk about your grandmother. What about your parents? Didn't you ever have parents?"

"A father, a mother, brothers, sisters, masses of them, masses. Everything you need to make a family. To populate the entire world. The only visible problem is the lack of room for sleeping. Three to a bed. Dresser drawers set on the floor. To sleep in. An air mattress in the tub. Diapers drying everywhere. On radiators. On lines strung up in the kitchen. Shot through with cries. I am shot through with cries. I didn't have a childhood. The first-born. Made to pick them up one by one as they come into the world. When my grandmother arrived, I'd been lying on a bed for three days as if I were dead. With my parents' approval she decided to adopt me. As soon as I was at my grandmother's, at her house in the country, along the very edge of the paved road, I settled into a peace like no other. At home, I was replaced right away. Scarcely two days after my departure, my fourteenth little sister was born, chubby and round. I've never heard her cries rip through the air above the rooftops. My grandmother was my nest. I'd never known anything like it. And I kept cheeping to go back to my nest and rest. I didn't return to the house in town, and no one in the family came to the country to see me at my grandmother's. Not my father, not my mother, not Malvina, who's going on six. Not Petit Louis or anything or anyone. All alone with my grandmother. For all eternity:"

Her voice monotonous, inexhaustible, lower and lower, muffled. Her story with no beginning or end. I'm becoming exasperated. And my own story down deep inside me is asking to be heard in turn. What a fine dialogue of the deaf Delphine and I would have. I cut short the preposterous idea of such a conversation. I take refuge in the kitchen till she falls silent and my soul does too.

Sleep overcame her as she lay in my bed with her long hair tangled and her clothes a mess.

I lie down beside her. Switch off the light. Listen to her slightly husky breathing in the dark.

The warmth of her sleeping body next to mine. It's so dark in the room that I can't see her face. I feel the desire to do with her what a man does with a woman in his bed. I kiss her lightly on the cheek. I touch her breasts under the T-shirt. She jumps up. Speaks very softly and with difficulty, as if each word were being wrenched from her.

"I'm living through a disaster, Édouard dear. Leave me alone. I followed Patrick Chemin like a dog. For days. Sometimes without seeing his face. Just an attraction, an odour that told me where he'd been. The first time, it was in a town of all levels and castes, the one where I was born. His eye, the eye of a sacred cow, had already ravaged me on the road, before he brought me with him to the hotel in town. I liked his little poor man's suitcases too. I bled a lot onto the hotel's sheets. Patrick Chemin washed them in the washbasin in the room. The water was all red. He kept saying: "Good God! What have I done?" I gave birth to a dead child and my love died at the same time as my child. Patrick Chemin is a pig. And you too, Édouard dear. Men are all alike. No more of that, ever. Now let me go."

The sound of a key turning in the lock. Middle of the night. Delphine has flung my door wide open on the landing. Goes slowly down the stairs. Her fatigue on her back like a stone.

What get in my way most are her suitcases; she left them on my rug and I have to walk around them to go from the bed to the table. As for the rest, I'll have to get used to those recurring images of her that make me shrink like an oyster reacting to drops of lemon juice.

Delphine anorexic amid the cheeping mob of her sisters and brothers, who are hungry for her. Delphine at the house of her grandmother, who is showing her how to tear a chicken leg to pieces with her teeth. The grandmother an ogress, Delphine an ogress in turn. The overwhelming love of the one and of the other. For the one and for the other. Grandmother and granddaughter.

Having not yet attained the point of absolute disappearance, the little ogress I found by the side of a fountain continues to eat into my time, to gnaw at my solitude. I can't bear not knowing where she is in the city. It's ten days now that she's been gone. But what can she be doing, with no money, no baggage, in a city crowded by all those people returning from their August vacations?

I look everywhere for her, with no hope, as if for a needle in a stack of hay.

Is it possible I'll find her mingling with the crowd on the *grands boulevards*, trailing behind the first man who comes along in the hope that he will turn around and assist her? I can't help thinking that even if her destitution became extreme, she wouldn't hold out her hand. She would never ask for charity. But she'd be so alone and lost that people would give her alms without her asking. No doubt she'd just have to be there on the sidewalk, waiting for the world to end, her eyes blank, her face pale and insulted, facing a stranger who would turn away, hounded by her for hours now, and she'd attract the most perverse compassion.

I've been walking since morning.

The city is spilled out abundantly around me. A smashed anthill. But shining in the lacklustre crowd, like lighted rallying points here and there, are anonymous joys, furtive rages.

No trace of Delphine.

All I can do is go home. Back to my stairs, my four walls, my catalogues.

Stéphane's mother is recovering slowly. Stéphane won't be back in Paris before next week. Marianne and Patrick are on Ile de Ré till September 15.

I damn myself all alone.

And now she has chosen this propitious time of my own damnation to perfect it in a way, to turn up at my place once again, and end her days in my bed.

A burst aneurysm, the autopsy report will declare.

III

E verything seems to be in order around me. The body removed. The bed made. The room aired out. All I have to do is resume my idiotic work, with complete peace of mind. It would take someone clever to get me out of here now. But here is her little voice, half worn away by the ravages of death, drawing me out of the opacity in which I've enclosed myself:

"Let me sleep here. Only sleep."

She, always she, Delphine. Not sleeping. Acting in secret. Consuming her life and her death amid hidden violence.

Let the frozen ocean spread out between us as far as the eye can see. The pole and its ice. Never walk across the empty space. Between her and me. Between myself and me, I should say. Myself, in the flesh. Childhood abolished, the wish for non-return. Adulthood as a desiccated fruit. Very little air around me. Just enough to breathe between the pages of a mail-order catalogue. Delphine is unwelcome. All compassion unwarranted. Such frost inside me. Such cold, unimaginable for a creature from a temperate country like the one where I happened to be born. Exquisite light of the country around Tours. The banks of the Loire sandy and mild. A father, a mother, planted there, inadvertently no doubt, in the midst of rich, level soil. And the second son, born to them too late, like a bitter root doomed to freeze.

Who talks about breaking the ice? Harsh, forbidden memory (unless it is little Delphine, acid and stubborn). With what highly sharpened axe? What effort on the part of the entire being who seizes the axe with both hands? If by chance I were able to break the frozen sea within me, I would have Delphine at my fingertips, alive and shuddering, and perhaps, as well, a little boy who was killed, who was caught in the ice in the depths of my night. Above all, I must not become emotionally involved. The risk of waking the still water is too great. I prefer to let the dead bury the dead, twenty thousand leagues beneath the sea. The real terror is that the shadow of God's pity should be well and truly lost in the depths of the accumulated gloom.

The greatest disturbance in the world — when the waters were divided from the firmament, with a crashing of foam and molten lava — would likely have had no more effect on me than Delphine, death at her back, climbing into my bed.

"Am I disturbing you?"

To silence Delphine. To exhaust with one stroke the words of the living woman, the silence of the dead woman. To prevent her from coming to me under the ice, like a little smelt. Let her be absolutely dead. Killed by me. Once and for all. Beyond any pity for her and for me.

Am I not free to rid myself of Delphine as something that's in my way? To sort out her images one at a time before I dump them overboard? Now I am settling her one last time on the edge of the Saint-Sulpice fountain. I leave her for a moment on a country road in a strange land. I push her into Patrick Chemin's arms. I cause Delphine's child to live or die at will under her pink dress. I hear the cries of the imaginary child before he returns to the limbo he should never have left. Delphine's gaze, so blue, slips through my fingers.

Nothing. Nothing more is happening under the transparent ice. Because I assure you that there is nothing alive here, only the pitiful episodes in Delphine's life and death, filing untidily towards the exit. A school of little fish good only for frying. Pointless to lean over the overflowing water. If minuscule eddies persist, their bubbles barely visible, it is only the end of imaginary abysses as they close up over strange, broken memories. Nothing. There is nothing more to see here. Only the echo of some lost words persists, pounds against my temple.

Sounds (nothing but sounds) loom up, syllables assemble and take pleasure in strange couplings. A little more and the words will come into view, sharp and clear; soon they will form complete sentences, and the meaning of the world, long since disappeared, cast back into the darkness, will become as clear as spring water dipped from the depths of the sea when its black crust is broken into pieces. A harsh memory split from top to bottom. I hear Madame Benoît testifying before the court of God:

"I swear it. That child's eyes are filled with tears."

Madame Benoît repeats the same thing again and again beneath the black ice. A very small fissure suffices, a mere thinning of the frozen surface, for the sound to come through. There is talk of a little boy with frozen tears as I find myself again at the age of five or ten.

This woman comes to visit my parents every Sunday, at the hour when they drink a pastis, and afterwards she drives away in her little violet Méhari, going down the roads of the country around Tours to gather up every sign of sorrow or grief for miles around.

And I, I, Édouard Morel — a forgetful man if ever there was one — am I to be placed forcibly in intimate contact with a whining child? Tender enough to die. Am I to be obliged to recognize myself in that child, the second-born of Rose and Guillaume Morel, cabinetmaker by trade? It's no small thing to place my feet in my own footsteps and say: There it is, it's me. Here is the house and the peaceful garden. The hydrangeas, blue on one side of the hedge and pink on the other because of the different soil my father transplanted there by the wheelbarrow load.

Neighbouring gardens, matching hydrangeas, identical houses arranged along a single line, tiny reference points for the great trains that travel across Saint-Pierre-des-Corps day and night. I am haunted by the trains of Saint-Pierre-des-Corps, their broad, fierce music that rends the air like long knives, their absolute energy, hurled from end to end of the living earth, which is furrowed as a field is furrowed by the plough. Under such a din I will see, no longer just hear, what is going on beneath the frozen memory, as if there were no past or present, not even a possible future, once it has been given over to forgotten words and gestures, while lost odours come along in fresh bunches. And I shall never again be free to exist on the surface of myself, like someone standing on a narrow balcony outside his house, with all the doors behind him closed like prison gates.

And if my mother's warmth were to waken, the gentle warmth of her tender, sweet, warm breast where I rest my cheek in dreams, my entire life would be returned to me at a stroke.

But now a series of small and unimportant facts swirls before my eyes like a swarm of gnats.

The odour of pale wood-shavings, eaten away by emanations of glue and varnish, envelops me from head to toe. My father bends over me. Examines me attentively.

"This child certainly doesn't look like the Other. Too dark. Too small."

My mother repeats, echoing him:

"Dear God, how dark he is! Dear God, how small he is! What a shame!"

Between her breasts, the medal worn smooth by the gentle rubbing of my mother's flesh. The Other, the First-born, lately dead, rests there in his unchanging innocence for an eternity of adoration and grief.

His blue eyes. His blond hair. First in his class. First at home. His unchanging qualities of an absolute First. The dead little child I replace. The Other. The daunting example. I may as well resign myself to not existing.

The sea has frozen over all that. God's pity sleeps at the very bottom, in a cold shadow.

I shave at the sink in my kitchen on Rue Bonaparte. A drop of blood stands out on my cheek. No one can know about the poor quality of my blood. First of all, it's perfectly normal blood. Rh positive. Like most inhabitants of the planet. Who can possibly know that one day when I was a child my vermilion blood was changed? Not all at once, but through a series of small bloodlettings. Not that it became blue or green or violet or any other surprising colour; it simply changed into other blood, natural-looking, unobjectionable, irreproachable at first sight, but in reality its very essence is corrupt. My own mediocrity slips through test tubes like some elusive virus. No bitter drama or thundering tragedy when this strange transfusion began. Trivialities at the origin of the world. Infantile behaviour. All traces gone, no sign of the frozen tears of my childhood. And if Delphine disturbs me, it is certainly because of those very tears, buried beneath the sea.

Death from natural causes, Dr. Jacquet will say. She will be repatriated to Canada. Don't worry about the baggage. The embassy will take care of everything.

Penelope's Way

Blanche Howard